398.2
P   Pevear, Richard
c.1   Mister Cat-and-a-
         half

DATE DUE		
Clement		

Mister
Cat-and-a-half

retold by
Richard Pevear

illustrated by
Robert Rayevsky

Macmillan Publishing Company
New York

Collier Macmillan Publishers
London

Macmillan Publishing Company
866 Third Avenue, New York, N.Y. 10022
Collier Macmillan Canada, Inc.
Printed and bound by
South China Printing Company, Hong Kong
First American Edition
10 9 8 7 6 5 4 3 2 1
The text of this book is set in Garamond No. 3.
The illustrations are rendered in ink and watercolor.

Concept and design by Vladimir Radunsky

Library of Congress Cataloging-in-Publication Data
Pevear, Richard, date.
Mister Cat-and-a-half.
Summary: A cat with a reputation for being fierce
is invited to dinner by the forest animals, where a
chain of accidents ensures the continuation of this
erroneous belief.
[1. Folklore–Soviet Union] I. Rayevsky,
Robert, ill. II. Title.
PZ8.1.P54Mi 1986 398.2'452974428'0947 [E] 85-18884
ISBN 0-02-773910-4

To Inna—R.R.

Once upon a time the royal kitchen was overrun with mice. The cook took in a starving cat, who proved to be an expert mouse catcher.

The cook was pleased. "I took in half a cat," he said, "and he turned out to be a cat and a half!"

The cat was even more pleased. It was not the work that he liked so much, but the milk and herrings and other treats the cook gave him. He grew sleek and fat and began to act more like king of the kitchen than like the cook's helper. He slept late in the mornings, sat all day in the sun, and helped himself to the royal supper at night.

The cook became annoyed. The cat would soon be eating as much as the mice had eaten. "Why should I keep such a do-nothing in my kitchen?" he said to himself. "I'll take him to the forest and leave him there." And so he did.

When the cat saw that he was alone, he sat down under a pine tree and wept. He had had such a good life, but for so short a time. He imagined how skinny and hungry he would soon be again.

What is more, he was afraid. He had never been in the forest. Every strange noise startled him, and all the noises were strange.

Suddenly a she-fox came trotting by. When she saw the cat, she stopped in amazement.

The cat was frightened. He arched his back and hissed, "Pfft! Pfft!" And his green eyes flashed.

The fox was impressed. "Who are you?" she asked. "And where do you come from?"

"I am Mister Cat-and-a-half," the cat replied. "I come from the royal palace."

"I am Mistress Fox, from the forest," said the fox, smiling as nicely as she could. She was delighted to have met such a fine gentleman. In truth, there were many creatures in the forest, but none of them was quite good enough for the fox. She had been waiting for a real gentleman to come along. And now here was Mister Cat-and-a-half!

The fox saw how sleek and fat the cat was and said, "Why don't we get married? I'll be a good wife to you. I'll see that you are well fed."

At that, the cat pricked up his ears. He took one more look at the forest around him and said, "All right."

So the fox gave him her arm, and they went to live in her house.

The fox did everything she could to please the cat. She would bring him a woodcock one day and a pheasant the next. She made sure he had enough to eat, even if she went hungry herself.

The cat soon decided that forest life was not so bad, after all. He slept late in the mornings and dozed in the sun all day.

One day the fox met her old neighbor, the wolf.

"Mistress Fox," said the wolf, "you are the finest lady in our part of the forest. I was just coming to ask you to marry me."

"No, no, do not even think of it!" said the fox. "I am already married to Mister Cat-and-a-half. If he sees you, he will tear you to pieces!"

"Oh!" said the wolf, who had never seen a cat and was frightened to have such a fierce animal for a neighbor. "In that case, is there some way I can make friends with him?"

"He likes fine food," said the fox. "Why don't you invite us to dinner?"

"Very well," said the wolf. And off he went into the forest.

Then the fox met her old neighbor, the bear.

"Mistress Fox," said the bear, "you are the finest lady in our part of the forest. I was just coming to ask you to marry me."

"No, no, do not even think of it!" said the fox. "I am already married to Mister Cat-and-a-half. If he sees you, he will tear you to pieces!"

"Oh!" said the bear, who had never seen a cat and was frightened to have such a fierce animal for a neighbor. "In that case, is there some way I can make friends with him?"

"He likes fine food," said the fox. "Why don't you invite us to dinner?"

"Very well," said the bear. And off he went into the forest.

Then the fox met her old neighbor, the boar.

"Mistress Fox," said the boar, "you are the finest lady in our part of the forest. I was just coming to ask you to marry me."

"No, no, do not even think of it!" said the fox. "I am already married to Mister Cat-and-a-half. If he sees you, he will tear you to pieces!"

"Oh!" said the boar, who had never seen a cat and was frightened to have such a fierce animal for a neighbor. "In that case, is there some way I can make friends with him?"

"He likes fine food," said the fox. "Why don't you invite us to dinner?"

"Very well," said the boar. And off he went into the forest.

The fox went home. At her door, she met her old neighbor, the hare.

"Mistress Fox," said the hare, "you are the finest lady in our part of the forest. Everyone says so. And so I have come to ask you to marry me."

"No, no," said the fox, "do not even think of it! I am already married to Mister Cat-and-a-half. If he sees you, he will tear you to pieces!"

Just then the cat stepped out the door. When he saw the hare, he arched his back and hissed, "Pfft! Pfft!" And his green eyes flashed.

The hare was so frightened that he dashed off into the forest without even saying good-bye to the fox.

The hare was still running when he came upon his old friends the wolf, the bear, and the boar.

"I saw him! I saw him!" cried the hare.

"Is he very big?" they asked.

"Big enough!" said the hare.

"What does he look like?"

"He arches his back," said the hare, "and he bristles all over, and his claws stick out, and he says 'Pfft! Pfft!' and his green eyes flash!"

"Woe to us!" cried his friends. "We are supposed to invite him to dinner!"

"Let's do it together," said the hare. "Then we'll be sure he has enough to eat. And with four of us, it will be safer!"

"But we've never made dinner for anyone before!"

"Never mind," said the hare. "Just do as I tell you. Wolf, you bring meat for the main course. Boar can root up potatoes. Bear can find fresh honey for dessert. And I will pick lettuce and carrots. We can all meet at my house."

They went their separate ways.

The hare quickly gathered armfuls of lettuce and carrots and brought them to his house. Soon the boar arrived. He was dragging a big sack of potatoes covered with dirt and roots. Then the wolf came, carrying a whole woolly ram on his back, horns and all.

After a while, they heard the crunch of heavy footsteps and a loud buzzing noise. The bear appeared, carrying a beehive at arm's length, with a long trail of angry bees behind him.

"Oh, my!" said the hare, and he sat holding his head.

"A fine beginning for a fine gentleman's dinner!"

But he soon put his friends to work. They washed and peeled and boiled and roasted, and they even managed to chase the bees away. At last everything was ready.

Then they began to argue over which of them would go to invite the fox and Mister Cat-and-a-half.

"I'm too fat," said the boar. "I'll get out of breath."

"I'm too slow," said the bear. "I'll be late."

"I'm too old," said the wolf. "I don't hear well."

Since there was no one else, the hare had to go. He ran to the fox's house and knocked three times on the window. *Tap-tap-tap!*

"What can I do for you?" asked the fox.

"The wolf, the bear, the boar, and I invite you and Mister Cat-and-a-half to dinner," said the hare. Then he bowed deeply, scraping the ground with his foot, and dashed away again.

The fox made herself ready, took Mister Cat-and-a-half by the arm, and off they went. As they walked through the forest, the cat puffed himself up and hissed, "Pfft! Pfft!" And his eyes flashed like two green lights.

The hare reached home, quite out of breath, and shouted, "They're coming! They're coming!"

The bear immediately climbed a tree.

The boar looked wildly around him and said, "I can't climb trees. Where shall I hide?"

"Get under the table," said the hare. And the boar squeezed under the table.

"What about me?" cried the wolf.

"Hide in that bush," said the hare. "I'll cover you up with leaves."

The wolf jumped into the bush, and the hare kicked leaves over him. Then the hare dove into a hole and sat there, shaking all over.

At that moment the fox and Mister Cat-and-a-half arrived for dinner. To their surprise, they found a table fully set with steaming plates of food, but there was no trace of their hosts.

As soon as the cat smelled the meat, he rushed to the table, crying, "Mrr-neow! Mrr-neow!"

The animals thought he was shouting "More now! More now!" and said to themselves, "What an appetite! He's already asking for more!"

Mister Cat-and-a-half ate his fill. Then he looked around for a place to lie down. Since there was nowhere else, he stretched out on the table.

The boar, crouched underneath, tried very hard not to move. He tried so hard that his tail began to twitch.

The cat mistook the tail for a mouse and pounced. When he saw the boar, the cat became so frightened that he ran up the nearest tree. It was the very tree the bear was hiding in.

The bear thought the cat was attacking him. He scrambled higher up the tree. But the branch got so thin that it broke under him, and he fell onto the bush where the wolf was hiding.

The wolf thought surely his end had come and ran for dear life. The bear and the boar ran, too. They ran so fast that the hare could not catch up with them.

When they finally stopped running, they huddled together in the forest, still shaking with fear, and said, "What an animal that one is! So small and yet so fierce! He almost ate us all up!"

Meanwhile, the fox and the cat sat down again and finished everything on the table.

As they rose to go, the fox said, "A fine dinner, Mister Cat-and-a-half. It's a pity our neighbors are so shy. They're not used to dining with a gentleman. But I'm sure they will invite us again."

And she and Mister Cat-and-a-half went home.